THE URBANA FREE LIBRARY

3 1230 00954 9268

W9-AXG-730

The Urbana Free Library
To renew: call 217-367-4057
or go to *urbanafreelibrary.org*
and select "My Account"

DISCARDED BY THE
URBANA FREE LIBRARY

To all the hardworking and dedicated teachers of civics, government, and American history. —M.F.

For Yujin and the better world to come. —V.K.

STERLING CHILDREN'S BOOKS
New York

An Imprint of Sterling Publishing Co., Inc.
1166 Avenue of the Americas
New York, NY 10036

STERLING CHILDREN'S BOOKS and the distinctive Sterling Children's Books logo are registered trademarks of Sterling Publishing Co., Inc.

Interior text © 2018 Martha Freeman
Illustrations © 2018 Violet Kim

All rights reserved. No part of this publication may be reproduced, stored in a retrieval system, or transmitted in any form or by any means (including electronic, mechanical, photocopying, recording, or otherwise) without prior written permission from the publisher.

ISBN 978-1-4549-2993-2

Distributed in Canada by Sterling Publishing Co., Inc.
c/o Canadian Manda Group, 664 Annette Street
Toronto, Ontario M6S 2C8, Canada
Distributed in the United Kingdom by GMC Distribution Services
Castle Place, 166 High Street, Lewes, East Sussex BN7 1XU, England
Distributed in Australia by NewSouth Books
45 Beach Street, Coogee, NSW 2034, Australia

For information about custom editions, special sales, and premium and corporate purchases, please contact Sterling Special Sales at 800-805-5489 or specialsales@sterlingpublishing.com.

Manufactured in China

Lot #:
2 4 6 8 10 9 7 5 3 1
05/18
sterlingpublishing.com

Interior and cover design by Heather Kelly

IF YOU'RE GOING TO A MARCH

by MARTHA FREEMAN

illustrated by VIOLET KIM

STERLING CHILDREN'S BOOKS
New York

If you're going to a march, you are going to want a sign.
A recycled pizza box works well.

Since you're going to be outside, be sure to check the weather. You'll want layers for cold, an umbrella for rain, or a hat and sunscreen for sunny days.

Wear sturdy, comfy shoes.

Travel light, but pack
snacks and water.

If your grown-ups choose to drive, parking may be tough.

You may want to walk or bike if it's not too far. Otherwise,
take the train or the bus or the subway.

You probably will not go by hot-air balloon,
but don't you wish you could?

So many people have come to the march!

Just like you, they are showing they care about their country and want to make things better.

Some people make speeches. They are excited and shouting.

Still, it's possible this part will get boring.

A march is serious business. But it's not healthy to be serious all the time. If there's music, feel free to cut loose and dance.

PROTEST IS PATRIOTIC

The speeches are over. The music is done.

IT'S TIME TO PICK UP
YOUR SIGN AND MARCH!

Double-knot your shoelaces so you don't trip. If you're careful, you won't get lost, but make sure you know your address and phone number.

You might have to use the bathroom.
If you do, give your sign to
someone to hold.

If you've made a friend, ask them to wait up.

There will be police officers at the march.
Their job is to keep people safe.
Some of them ride bikes.

There will be reporters, too. Their job is to tell the truth.
If you want to answer their questions, speak in a loud, clear voice.
There will be cameras everywhere. It's okay to smile.

LOVE & HOPE

LOVE OUR EART

FREE

NEWS

TE HOME

PEACE begins with ME

If your legs get tired, you can hitch a ride.

While you march, you will probably chant. Good chants are "Show me what democracy looks like! This is what democracy looks like!" and "The people united will never be defeated!" There are plenty more.

If you see people who disagree, be polite. Sometimes democracy looks like disagreement, too.

Maybe you will sing a good old protest song like "We Shall Overcome." Look around at your family, your friends, and your neighbors singing. Strangers are singing, too—all of you together, all of you caring.

Now you know for sure why you came to march today:

THERE'S A WARM FEELING IN YOUR HEART.

At last, it's time to go home.

You'll wish for that hot-air balloon.

Later, you'll be tired but happy. Today you showed everyone you care.
You did something good for your country.

Don't let your markers dry out, though. And keep saving pizza boxes.

YOU WILL WANT TO BE READY FOR NEXT TIME.

AFTERWORD

In the United States of America, we, the people, are in charge of government. This means we, the people, have to tell government what we want. When you're an adult you can do this by voting and running for office, but anyone of any age can protest and march.

There are many examples of protests throughout America's history. In the early twentieth century, protests helped women gain the right to vote.